SWOLE: WET WEDNESDAY

Published and written by: Golden Czermak
1st Edition

WARNING: This is a **short story** written for mature readers. It is pure

escapism, containing adult themes, coarse language, erotic sexual

situations, male-male sex, and nudity.

ACKNOWLEDGEMENTS

As always thank you to all my gym bros for inspiring this series. Apparently, the books require a subscription to Adam & Eve because they are so hot! Emma – one is headed your way!

SWOLE

WET WEDNESDAY

CHAPTER 1

MONDAY FUN DAY

AS JONNY CAMERON OPENED HIS eyes, the darkness slowly diminished, his view filling with a blur of colors that sharpened into an all-too-close view of an overly wrinkled pillow. He blinked a couple of times, and while wiping away a little bit of sleep from the corner of his eye, his nostrils flared. Hints of body wash and cologne swirled in, a memento of his latest encounter with the manly Trent Cassidy at his gym, Swole.

Damn he smells amazing…

That was all Jonny could think of as he tried to move into a more comfortable position. Quickly, he realized there wasn't one. With each awkward twist and turn he was reminded of how much of a dick Trent was (or at least how well he could use the big one that resided between his legs).

While on his stomach, Jonny stretched one of his slim arms back and grabbed a hefty chunk of his ass, massaging it beneath his fingertips. Letting out a moan, he didn't care how strange it looked – not that anyone could see him – but it was much needed relief from the pummeling Trent had delivered both on and in the squat rack the night before. His other hand soon joined the first, kneading the other cheek, and together they spread them apart. His fingers then slid their way toward his hole, invitingly exposed, while his cock started to swell against the futon mattress.

Oh God... Jonny thought, groaning.

A single finger danced across his sensitive skin, ready to breach.

Unhurriedly, it began to enter that warm, tight tunnel and Jonny's breathing quickened.

His eyes started to roll back and…

BUZZ! BUZZ! BUZZ!

"Jesus Christ!" Jonny yelled, shocked into reality by the alarm.

BUZZ! BUZZ! BUZZ!

An arm whipped out to the cluttered end table serving as a nightstand, knocking over an empty plastic cup. Jonny snatched his phone and gave it a deadly stare. The numbers staring back uncaringly indicated that it was sixty thirty in the morning.

"What on Earth were you thinking setting that so early?" Jonny snipped, mashing the alarm button.

As the app closed, he noticed there were a couple of missed text messages. His obsessive-compulsiveness took over, having to check them immediately.

They were from his friend Jared, who also happened to be Trent's roommate. While Trent and Jonny were at Swole 'working out' their legs, Jared had gone over to a local frat house to kick off spring break with a twelve-ounce bang.

Jonny scanned the litany of short messages, most an assortment of emojis and sentiments indicating how much Jared wanted Jonny. Despite their drunken and rather explicit nature, the words managed to bring a smile to Jonny's face; Jared was actually thinking about him while at the party, surrounded by guys that were probably much hotter and way more willing to drop their pants for a beastly romp. Jonny happily continued reading, his smile growing as the texts got less legible. When he reached the last message, his mouth suddenly dropped and his eyes widened.

It was a picture of Jared, wearing a grin as large as the one Jonny had just been. His wild hair had been slightly tamed with hair gel and his obnoxiously tight shirt had a deep neck scoop that showed off the top of his well-developed chest. It must have been warm out, each slab of striated muscle glistening with sweat. But it wasn't the chest or veiny, oversized biceps about to tear through the fabric that caught Jonny's attention. It was the can of beer Jared was holding down in front of his jeans, or rather what was next to it. Off to the left was a bulge so large that it looked like Jared had shoved an extra beer can down the front of them.

Now Jonny had seen Jared shirtless and in sweats before, so it wasn't a surprise that he was a big boy all over. Yet, there was something about the carefree attitude of *this* picture, coupled with the obvious hard-on Jared was packing beneath the denim, that started Jonny's dry lips smacking.

Well, I might as well take care of this, Jonny thought as he rolled himself onto his back.

Kicking away the covers, his dick popped free of its confines and surged to full size. Jonny reached down for it, wrapping his fingers firmly around the unyielding shaft.

"This is gonna be good," he mumbled, lustfully staring at the picture while biting his lower lip.

However, before he could pump out the first stroke, a flurry of noise came crashing through the crack in the guest room door.

"Motherfucker!" Jared's deep voice boomed from downstairs.

Jonny immediately let go of his cock, slamming the now empty fist onto the futon.

"I can already tell what kind of day this is going to be," he groaned, rising irritably to his feet. "Monday fun day…"

JONNY TRAIPSED DOWN THE STAIRS, the last couple of steps creaking loudly. He rounded the corner and entered the kitchen, spying the coffee machine sitting on the far counter before noticing Jared over at the sink. The stocky guy was wearing nothing but a tight pair of briefs that matched the blue of his eyes, though eyes were the last thing Jonny was staring at.

"You okay?" Jonny asked as he walked by, admiring the well-formed curves of Jared's body. Reaching the cabinets, he opened them and pulled out a large coffee cup.

"Yeah, I'm fine," Jared replied groggily, scratching at his messy hair.

"That's good. You were making quite the commotion, so wanted to be sure," Jonny said, inserting a coconut-flavored coffee pod into the machine before switching it on. "You managed to wake me up, you know?"

"Sorry about that princess; a stack of Trent's shaker cups fell off the drying rack into the sink. I tried to stop them, but my coordination's a bit... off this morning. I had a rough night."

"You certainly look it."

Jared squinted at Jonny, trying to be intimidating but it just made him look even more hungover and constipated.

"Well at least you had fun," Jonny added, "even if I wasn't there."

"You *should* have been," Jared replied sternly. "I wanted you there and would've enjoyed it a lot more. But, I'm sure you had other, better things to fill your time."

As his eyes anxiously scanned the room, Jonny thought he heard Jared mutter the name Trent and he really didn't feel like getting into it over him yet again. Thankfully, a little red light on the coffee machine caught his attention. Jonny pressed a small button just below it and watched as dark, steaming liquid started to fill his cup.

"I don't know about that," he said at last.

"Whatever, Jonny."

Jared's tone was harsh, made more so by his hangover, but Jonny took it in stride.

As the coffee finished pouring, Jonny took a sip, finding it too hot. He blew across the top of the cup as he walked into the living room and on toward the back of the house.

"Jonny, I…" Jared called out, but his words fell on deaf ears. Frustrated, he followed, footsteps loud on the wood floor. "Hey, wait a second!"

Jonny hadn't gotten too far, standing in front of a wall of windows. Sheer, tan drapes ran from corner to corner and just on the other side, a pair of French doors led to a balcony that overlooked a sea of evergreen trees that surrounded the hilltop home. He reached out for the door knob, but Jared stopped him with a firm grip on the forearm.

"Ow!" Jonny protested.

"Shit, I… I'm sorry," Jared said with a much softer voice, loosening his hold but not letting go. "Look, I shouldn't have stormed off last night."

"It's no biggie; seems like your text messages more than made up for that."

"Yeah, well, I'm regretting sending those, too. Standing here, I can't shake the feeling that you've made your choice, Jonny."

"Choice?"

"Yeah, a choice named Trent. I'm just complicating matters by continuing to push this. It's only confusing the fuck out of you… and me."

Jonny took a swig of coffee, now at a tolerable temperature.

"As much as I want to agree with you, that's not entirely the case. I'm contributing just as much to this back and forth as you and yeah, it's confusing. Hell, it seems the only thing I *am* certain of right now is how *un*certain and abnormal the situation is."

"Shit, that's the understatement of the year," Jared chuckled.

"More like the century," Jonny pegged on, pausing when he saw a hopeful look spread across Jared's face.

"So, wait," Jared started. "What you're telling me is that there's still a chance for you and I? After all of this?"

Jonny took in a deep breath and sighed.

"Again, I wish it were as clean cut as that, but it's not black and white. You're going to be stuck with angsty Jonny until I can figure all this out for myself."

"I'm okay with that. An angsty boy is better than no boy at all," said Jared reassuringly. "Even if he comes in thirty shades of gray."

"It's fifty…"

"What is?" Jared asked.

"The… oh, never mind," Jonny answered, sputtering. Changing the subject, he continued with, "Maybe it was too soon for me to come down after breaking up with Fred. I knew damn well that *something* was going to happen, just not with Trent."

"That's because you didn't even know he existed and he basically swept himself in like the doucher he is. Unlike someone else you know…"

Jonny glanced over and saw that Jared still looked like he was waiting on pins and needles.

"True, and… fine! The short answer is yes," Jonny finally said. "You and I still have potential. A lot of it, in fact."

Jared smiled at the reply, tempering his happiness with a head shake. As he let go of Jonny's arm, he noticed a fleeting look in his friend's eyes. Just then, he had an epiphany. Like a book had been opened, Jared was able to read exactly what Jonny was getting out of all this, or so his best guess at it.

Planning to find out if he was correct, Jared eased himself closer and bore his blue eyes into Jonny's brown ones.

"We're both quite fucked up, you know?"

"Speak for yourself," Jonny said gently as he leaned in. Their lips nearly touched as he grasped for the doorknob.

With Jared's help, Jonny's hand wrapped around the cool metal, twisted it, and opened the door. The morning air had some bite, flowing over both men's skin and causing it to prickle.

Jonny tried to pull himself away, but Jared had placed his other hand on the back of his neck, stopping him.

"I *am* speaking for myself," Jared answered, pressing his lips against Jonny's as the sun peeked through the pine needles. "Especially when I say that I'm really happy to have you here."

JARED AND JONNY STOOD NEXT to each other on the balcony as the sun continued to rise. Jared's thick arm had made its way around Jonny's upper back, while his fingers caressed Jonny's shoulder before sweeping down to his lower back.

Jonny found himself content and unprotesting, staring off at the brightening sky as if in a daydream.

"I guess we should get on with this day," Jared whispered as he shifted uncomfortably, his voice breaking though the sound of rustling branches and birdsong that had filled the last fifteen minutes.

"Can't we just stay here all day," Jonny mumbled, though he knew they had plans to tend to. He wriggled free of Jared, stepping a few paces down the balcony to give himself ample room to stretch. "Mondays suck no matter the occasion, don't they?"

"Yeah and the beaches are going to be extra sucky today, too. Very overcrowded. Not that I'm against all that skin and seaside fun, but I'd really like to spend some one-on-one time with you away from it all."

To some that might have been boring, but Jonny thought it sounded quite nice; a different pace than what he'd grown accustomed to with work, school, and life in general. Not to mention his frenetic, late night gym sessions.

"I'd really like that," Jonny said with a smirk as the door jostled, then opened behind them.

"Like what?" asked a voice rimmed with sleep.

It was Trent, stumbling out into the daylight but looking like he should have stayed in the dark for a few more hours. Shading his eyes with one hand, he attempted to groom himself with the other.

Jonny stiffened up at the sight of him.

Jared just stared apprehensively.

"Good morning Cassidy," Jared said curtly, noting Trent was wearing nothing but a jock strap. He didn't have much room to say anything, though, considering his own attire. "I could have sworn you said that you had clients this morning. Figured you'd be at Swole by now, charming your way into them."

Trent arched an eyebrow, the grunt he let out becoming a yawn as he rubbed his washboard stomach.

"Oh, my bad. I meant to say at Swole by now, being charming *to* your clients," Jared corrected.

Trent grunted again.

"That was the original plan, but my first client canceled and the second one gave me a heads up that she was going to be late," he replied, only to yawn again. Grabbing hold of his junk, he didn't hesitate to adjust it right there in front of the two of them. "That first bitch is causing me all sorts of issues. I think she's also chatting to her friends. She's one strike away from getting cut out of the program entirely and losing all her money. I can work out a deal with the second one."

"I've no doubts that you can," Jared replied flippantly, but Trent wasn't paying him any attention.

"So, Jonny-boy," Trent said cockily, "do you have any fun things planned for today?"

Jonny nodded, pointing over in Jared's direction.

"Yessir," he said almost sheepishly, "spending the day with him."

Jared's chest puffed up at the recognition while Trent's abs seemed to flex harder than before.

Jesus guys, Jonny thought. *What are you, peacocks?*

"So, it looks like you're leaving the real fun for the evening hours, then?" Trent said in a low voice.

Jared scoffed, he and Trent staring at each other for what seemed like hours when only seconds ticked by. Jonny could feel his heart beating faster, hoping they didn't break out into a fight, although a part of him would not have minded two obscenely muscular guys fighting in their underwear right in front of him.

"Well you two have fun today," Trent said calmly, seeming to diffuse the tension. It didn't last. "I have to get ready for work and training whatever clients actually decide to show up. Some people like J-rod here don't have to bust ass, since Mommy and Daddy are footing the college bills."

"That leaves me more time to better myself, bro," Jared retorted. "Something you could do. There's more to life than just lifting weights and lining up my next pretty training victim to be a warm sleeve to shove my dick in each night."

Damn, Jonny thought, those words hitting him squarely in the chest (or ass, depending on how he took what Jared was saying).

"Present company excluded of course," Jared added quickly, speaking across his shoulder.

Jonny paused; he didn't feel excluded, watching as the two men continued their ridiculous bouts of alpha preening. The truth was that he was the cause, right smack in the middle of it.

"You know what would be a lot easier?" Jonny blurted out. "Just whipping your cocks out to see whose is bigger."

Before the words had even stopped coming out of his mouth, Jonny realized he'd opened the door to more shit.

Trent coughed assuredly and immediately yanked down his jock strap. He slid his hand over and grabbed hold of the base of his cock, spinning it around like a helicopter.

Planting his face right into his soft palms, Jonny listened as Jared laughed. He swore he could also hear Trent's dick swishing its way through the air.

"What are we, twelve?" Jared asked as he casually folded his arms behind his neck.

"Twelve inches more like."

"You damn well wish you were," Jared snarled. "I gather you actually want to sword fight now, too?"

"Fuck off, J-rod. You'd never get close enough to it."

"Lucky for you, since my club would easily dent that toothpick you call a dick."

"Being thicker is not always better, boyo," Trent said as he spun around and started to walk back inside, bare ass waving goodbye with each step.

"I bet nine out of ten people would beg to differ, the tenth being dead," Jared tossed out, but Trent didn't take the bait.

"You kids enjoy the rest of your day," Trent replied, luring Jonny's face out of his hands. Trent glanced over his shoulder and winked at him. "As for you, Jonny-boy, I'll see you later on. Unfortunately, these client issues need my attention tonight, so back training day's delayed. Be ready though, a day off means I'm going to work you extra hard."

Jared snickered at the emphasis Trent placed on key words and once the door was fully closed, Jonny stood still for a moment. He didn't know if he should look over at Jared, but ultimately risked a peek.

"What in God's name was *that*?" Jared asked once their eyes met, letting loose a hearty chuckle. "I've never seen him like this over anyone."

"I've no idea," Jonny replied, "but I don't think that's the last time we'll be seeing Trent's wang."

"Well I don't plan on seeing it anytime soon, though *you'll* apparently be seeing it later this week," Jared said menacingly. "Be… ready… for… *hard*… work."

"Oh, stop it!" Jonny barked.

He didn't like being treated like a child in middle of a raging custody battle, yet he also realized that he held most – if not all – of the cards.

CHAPTER 2

GROWING BONDS

JONNY AND JARED SPENT MOST of the morning recuperating from their encounter with Trent Jr., but as unexpected as the event was, there was a silver lining. Trent's dick, out of all the things in the world, managed to give them something to talk about and the two of them grew closer as the day went on. Getting some light shopping in, then watching a matinee showing of the latest blockbuster, the morning quickly transitioned into afternoon.

Jared was having a great time, but the streets were incredibly crowded, hardly conducive to his plans for one-on-one time with Jonny. Even the public parks, normally vacant or populated with a few dog walkers, were overflowing with out-of-towners seeking somewhere to relax since the beaches were a veritable mess. The hunt was on for somewhere quiet and after a few phone calls, Jared found a solution.

"Where were we were going?" Jonny asked from the passenger seat of Jared's Maserati as it glided down a stretch of tree-lined road on the outskirts of town.

The trip was notably smoother than what he'd experienced the last two nights in Trent's Charger, but Jonny suspected rough rides and Trent came hand in hand, all those puns perfectly fitting.

"I'm taking us to a lookout called Juniper Point. It's the only place with easy access I could come up with, short of the balcony at the house, where we can get to know each other a little better." Jared's voice was calm, his left hand perched atop the steering wheel. "Plus, we shouldn't have any interruptions."

Jonny looked over, casually following Jared's vascular forearm toward his biceps, free of restraints in a tight tank top.

"Looks awesome…" he murmured, causing Jared to smirk. "I mean, that *sounds* awesome. So, um… yeah. How'd you find out about this place?"

"My buddy Greg told me about it. Greg Olden; he's the last one I was on the phone with."

"The one I could hear without the phone being on speaker?"

"Yeah, that's him; enthusiastic for sure. He's an avid, um, huntsman if you will, interested in a lot of that supernatural mumbo-jumbo. He actually goes looking for it on the weekends."

Jonny grinned uneasily.

"Weird as all that shit sounds," Jared continued, "it takes him to a lot of cool places, this lookout being one of them. Now, it *is* on some private property, but he cleared it with the owners so we should have privacy and no trespassing worries. Apparently, the coastal view is incredible."

Jonny was still stuck on the supernatural part.

"So, what you're saying is the amazing view is the last thing we'll see before being murdered by some monster? I hope it's a werewolf."

"Haha, we'll be fine," Jared smiled. "Besides, Greg said we only have to worry about the area once every twenty-seven years. I think that particular anniversary is sometime *next* week, so you'll be fine."

Jonny's lips turned down so fast it looked like he had given birth to a stack of bricks.

"I'm joking," Jared emphasized.

"Uh huh, sure you are," Jonny spat, diverting his attention back outside.

He was eager about getting there, even though he had no idea where they were going. The supernatural part *was* a little unnerving, especially since the woods seemed to go on forever, darkening in a creepy way that could make anyone, even Trent, feel uncomfortable.

Jared could tell Jonny was a bit perturbed.

"Hey, look back there real quick; I have a surprise for you," Jared directed calmly. Lifting a hand, he popped a thumb toward the rear seats.

Jonny twisted around, the soft leather enveloping his body. He spotted what looked like a large picnic basket – wicker and everything – tucked snuggly under a zip-up hoodie.

"You've got to be joking."

"What?" Jared replied innocently.

"When did you find the time to sneak all that in the car?"

"I..."

"You know what? Never mind, I don't want to ruin the mystery."

"What can I say, I'm a romantic at heart and where there's a will..."

"There's a way, eh?" Jonny finished. "That's all well and good, Jared, but a *picnic?*"

"Yeah, a picnic!" he countered. "Are you saying a beefcake and his nerd can't drive out into the country for one?"

"When you put it like *that*, who can argue?" Jonny replied, giggling as he smoothed out the wrinkles in his *Mario* tee. "So, Fabio, how much longer until we arrive?"

Jared glanced from the road to an ornate analog clock in the dashboard, then back again.

"Shouldn't be long now."

SURE ENOUGH, AFTER FIVE OR so minutes, a gravel road emerged from the shrubbery on the left. Flicking on the indicator, Jared made his way onto the narrow drive, passing a small sign that read 'Private

Property'. There were a few shallow dips that followed and a long, snaking curve, all leading deeper into the ominous woods.

"You sure this is the right way?" Jonny asked, gulping as he lost sight of the sky for all the trees.

He could swear his mind was playing tricks on him with all distant and shadowy shapes looming in the forest. Thankfully, before he could dwell too much on it, the vehicle emerged into a picturesque, grassy clearing.

"Here we are," Jared said as he stopped the car in a circular area large enough to turn around.

Jonny looked out ahead and saw a majestic cliff, stunning clouds rolling peacefully above while the sea crashed energetically against the rocks below.

"Wow, you weren't kidding," Jonny said breathlessly, his panic replaced with awe. "It's beautiful here."

"That it is, man. That it is."

Opening the door, Jonny was the first to step out. Making his way to the front of the car, gusts of wind rippled through his clothes and hair, while the crisp smell of the sea filled his nostrils.

Jared wasn't far behind, making sure to snag the basket from the back seat. Unhurriedly, he walked up behind Jonny, his arm finding a place around him before leading them to the cliff face.

Jonny started to feel a sprinkling of salt spray across his face.

"I think this is close enough," he said anxiously. "I don't think we need to get drenched."

"Not yet anyway," Jared replied boldly, digging into the basket while his tongue poked out of the corner of his mouth. Out came a large, patterned blanket that had been haphazardly folded. Spreading it out on the grass, it wasn't any neater. Nonetheless, Jared waved his hand invitingly across the wrinkled fabric. "After you, sir."

Jonny kneeled while Jared stayed upright. From the lower angle, he looked even bigger than usual.

"I could get used to this," Jonny told him, looking up reverently.

"Me too," Jared replied, hand already back in the basket. He pulled out a large Styrofoam container and offered it to Jonny.

"What's this?"

"Lunch, of course," Jared answered and once Jonny had taken hold, he pulled out another one for himself before taking a seat. "Wouldn't be much of a picnic without food."

"Uber fancy," Jonny said, opening the container. Inside was a burger, pickle, the tiniest container of coleslaw, and fries.

"What, you were expecting fine china teaming with caviar and truffles?"

"Don't forget the crystal glassware filled to the brim with wine."

"My, aren't you the sneaky little diva?"

"No, just being a nerd. Figured I would deduce the quality of lunch based on the luxury level of your car."

"Touché," said Jared. He pulled out two packets of plastic cutlery, tossing one over to Jonny. "I'll make up for it later. Here's the silverware, boo. Spared no expense."

They laughed, Jared studying Jonny intimately as they ate; every nuanced move and expression amplified in the warm sun despite the ample breeze. It was then that Jared felt something beyond mere flesh, the brown eyes, and hair.

Fascinating, he thought privately while crunching down on his pickle.

Jonny smiled, the obnoxious noise causing him to cough.

Jared could see that all the innocent geekiness, mixed with a deviant sexual side, made for an explosive mix. He thought on it more, sensing he wasn't far off in his earlier assumptions. Jonny was likely using

Trent, just as much as Trent was using him, each for their own raw,

physical pleasure. On the other hand, Jared offered something Trent

couldn't: emotional support. Lighthearted as they were being over Jared's

romantic nature, there was something to be said about things being *more*

than physical between two people; especially these two.

The duo carried on eating for some time, surrounded by nature

and enjoying each other's company.

"J-rod," Jonny asked, the cough still tormenting the back of his

throat, "do you have anything in that big basket of yours to drink?"

Jared held up a finger, chewing a couple more times before

mumbling, "One sec."

Rummaging around while Jonny felt like he was about to

suffocate, Jared produced a small bottle of water, followed by an equally-

sized bottle of whiskey. Holding them both up, they glinted in the sun like

prized trophies.

Jonny's eyes darted to and fro, picking the water to wash down all

the caked-up carbs. Snatching it out of Jared's hand, he twisted off the cap

and downed nearly half of it at once.

"No, no, leave that out," he called; Jared had started to put the whiskey away. Setting down his container of food and the water, he moved himself closer. "There's always time for dessert."

"It's five o'clock some…" Jared started to say, stopping when Jonny kissed him.

It wasn't long after that when Jonny's hands removed Jared's tank top, exploring his beefy body. They traced each vein, ran along every ripple, and caressed each muscle.

Jared could feel Jonny pressing against his chest, fingers teasing his hardening nipples. He could have resisted easing himself back, but didn't. Continuing to coax passion from Jonny's lips, Jared reclined until he was fully horizontal.

No sooner than Jared's bare back touched the blanket, Jonny clambered on top of him like a meaty mountain, taking off his own shirt. His hands found a new home on Jared's torso. There, Jonny's fingers fell into the large channel that ran down the center of his friend's abs, and quicker than a flash, his tongue headed that way. The divide was deep, Jonny lapping excitedly at both sides of the hard valley it formed.

God, it was so hot, the sun eclipsed by the heat radiating off their bodies.

Filled with lustful thirst, Jonny reached out and grabbed hold of the whiskey bottle. Before he knew it, he was pouring the amber liquid onto Jared as if his body was a shot glass. The divot filled quickly then overflowed, sending golden streams down his smooth skin. Jonny caught what he could with his tongue so it didn't go to waste. Then, positioning himself over the makeshift bowl, he sucked down every drop, licking the area clean before refilling it.

"Damn, boy," Jared whispered, his cock rising in his jeans, stretching the denim

"Ah, there it is," Jonny said eagerly, recalling the photo he was texted the night before. "Now, I'm not normally a beer guy, but I think I can make an exception for this can…"

"Fuck," said Jared achingly slow. "I need you to take it out."

"Yeah?"

"Oh, yeah. It's getting too tight in there."

"Literally too big for your own britches?" Jonny prodded.

"You're about to find out," Jared replied with a slight grimace. "I wasn't kidding with Trent… I want to see you try and take it."

"*Try?*" Jonny scoffed, working to unbutton the jeans. "Is that a challenge?"

Jared didn't answer immediately, only raising his eyebrows.

Jonny spread the denim apart.

"You bet it is," Jared chuckled. "Just use your mouth; I don't want to cripple you. Today at least."

Jonny could feel himself getting wet, his dick literally drooling at the sound of that deep voice. It caused his body to tremble in all sorts of wrong ways. Then he saw it: Jared's cock in all its glory. The thing was massive.

"Holy. Fucking. Shit," Jonny mouthed, yet no sound came.

Observing the meat that pulsated restlessly before him, Jonny advanced on it. Cautiously, he brought the head right up to his lips, finding the first stream of precum just what he was looking for. Downing it like a whiskey chaser, more replaced it, soon flowing like water from a faucet.

"Oh yeah, that's it," Jared growled. "I want you to take…"

His words were cut off when Jonny forced his lips around the head. It barely fit inside his mouth, his aching hands faring better as they stroked the eight by eight-inch beast.

As he worked, Jonny couldn't help but wonder what this gargantuan thing would feel like inside him. Trent had managed to make him sore with what *he* had between his legs, so Jared's dick would probably

split him wide open and then send him a bill for the privilege.

"O…oh… G-God," Jared stammered, breaths quickening.

Jonny kept going, the moaning spurring him on even though his

jaw was about to cramp around all that slippery flesh.

"B-baby, unless y-you want to drown I suggest…"

But Jared had already passed the point of no return, sending ropes

of hot cum surging into Jonny's mouth. It choked him as Jared watched

with a confident grin. Placing his hands on the back of Jonny's head, Jared

held him firm like the cock being gagged on, white streams pouring down

the entire shaft like melted ice cream.

Jared let go.

"Good God!" Jonny gasped.

"I tried to warn you," said Jared, grabbing hold of Jonny's

shoulders. He guided him up and stole a sticky kiss.

"A little late for that," Jonny replied, wiping away some excess cum

from the corner of Jared's mouth with a thumb.

Jared shrugged as he licked it off, grabbing hold of Jonny's

erection.

"As they say: better late than never," Jared said nonchalantly. "And by the looks of things, it's your turn now, Jonny-boy."

CHAPTER 3

GETTING SWOLE AGAIN

THE REST OF MONDAY FLEW by like the flock of distant birds soaring ahead of an oncoming storm. The clouds above Juniper Point were getting thicker and the air was cooling down, but that didn't deter Jared nor Jonny from laying, unbothered, in each other's arms. Perhaps it was their budding feelings which kept them there for nearly two blissful hours, but more than likely it was the exhausting, cum-filled picnic they'd had.

Jared was the first to wake from their nap; sprinkles of something wet were hitting his face.

"Jonny, not right now..." he groaned playfully, scratching at his stubble before raising his eyelids.

Greeted by rain instead of the penis he was expecting, Jared laughed, wishing they could have stayed longer in the idyllic setting. However, the weather insisted otherwise, and with a soft thump to the shoulder an irritable Jonny was roused.

"Hey there sleepy-head," Jared whispered beneath the sound of thunder. "We've got to go before..."

Large sheets of rain started to cascade across the clearing, and Jonny's eyes shot open to full size. With a sudden burst of energy, the two of them scrambled to collect their belongings. Racing to the Maserati with items loosely in hand, they threw it all into the back and plopped their soaked asses into the front seats.

The leathery squeaking was soon overcome by the roar of rain and as the visibility outside dropped, Jonny looked over to Jared.

"That was a close call," Jonny said. He licked his lips as a drop of water crested the upper one.

"No kidding," Jared answered, stretching out his arm. He playfully teased Jonny's sopping hair. "I much prefer getting soaked by you..."

"Don't go and get yourself *too* dry then," Jonny advised, "and I'll promise there'll be more to come later."

Jared cranked the engine, revving it twice.

"Good to hear," he said, glancing quickly at this phone. As the car started moving, he continued, "To think, I get you all to myself. Well, at least until tomorrow night."

"Can't find any fault with that," Jonny said with a hint of surprise; Jared seemed so complacent about the handoff to Trent.

Speaking of the brute, Trent had left a couple of text messages with Jared, asking him to drop by the supplement store to pick up some more pre-workout (and Jonny couldn't help but blush as he remembered why). The rest of Trent's messages indicated he would be busy addressing his mounting business issues.

"What that probably means," Jared translated, "is some jaded women and men found out about the other jaded women and men Trent's been 'comforting'."

Jonny smirked, looking back outside. Gaps formed in the rain sheets, and Jonny realized the woods that had been so ominous earlier – even now under a dark and stormy sky – weren't too bad after all. In fact, his fears had been replaced by memories as bright as the sun, filled by the scruffy face of a great friend who was rapidly becoming more.

TUESDAY MORNING ARRIVED AND A loud noise woke Jonny with a start. Jared's snoring was the culprit, filling the room with rumble that was probably setting set off the new seismometers connected to the university's Earth Sciences department.

Jonny crunched forward, lifting his head slightly. Looking around at the sheets of Jared's bed, they were rough and wrinkled from a night of unabridged fuckery. They would have still been going at it, the only thing stopping them from doing more was Jonny's poor dick, aching to the point of retreat after its third time getting off. On the other hand, Jared had no issues after four times, a fifth likely a breeze for the thick beast.

Settling back into the pillow, Jonny raised an arm and placed it across his forehead. Staring at the smooth, white ceiling, his mind started drifting despite the noise, wondering if Trent would blow a gasket if he knew what had gone down (and up, and down again) under that roof. The two of them were hardly quiet, so he definitely would've heard them taking full advantage of the lack of rules Jared imposed about 'interactions' at home. That was certainly a factor that allowed their feelings to flourish more than Jonny expected.

It didn't stop as the day progressed, either.

After a while, Jared must've stopped snoring and Jonny slipped back into sleep. It was then that Jared opened his eyes, finding Jonny drooling down his neck onto the pillow.

"You up?" Jared asked in a low voice, not really wanting to wake him. There was no reply, and something that he wanted to do.

Shuffling his way out of bed, Jared tiptoed from the room and headed downstairs. He slid against the wall, gliding over the bottom steps so they didn't creak too much. At the base, he craned his neck to check Trent's room at the end of the hall. The door was wide open, the room dark save for streams of light filtering in through the venetian blinds. There was no sign of Trent inside and from what Jared could make out, the bed hadn't been slept in.

I wonder where Casanova Cassidy is or who he's in, he wondered, but instead of dwelling on it, Jared brushed it off and continued into the kitchen. There was someone upstairs requiring his attention.

Rifling through the cabinets and the fridge, he gathered a couple of pans, utensils, and ingredients to make a simple but romantic meal. Cooking was unquestionably *not* his forte, so the fact he escaped with only a tiny cut on his index finger and light burn on his thumb was a miracle. Feeling mighty proud of himself, Jared then plated the food before loading it all onto a cutting board. Using it like a tray, he marched back upstairs.

"What's this?" Jonny asked as Jared entered, woken by the irresistible smell of bacon.

Jonny sat up to get a better look and Jared set the cutting board gingerly on Jonny's lap.

"Breakfast in bed, my man. *Oeufs et bacon en croute*," he said with a thick French accent and a huge grin across his face, all while twizzling the corner of a long and non-existent mustache.

"You mean bacon and eggs," Jonny reacted plainly, "on toast?"

Jared chuckled, then slumped forward.

"Well shit, Jonny," he said, shrugging his boulder-like shoulders. "When you put it *that* way, it loses something in translation."

"It doesn't lose as much as you'd think," Jonny replied, teasing his fingers through Jared's spiky hair. "It's still amazing. Just like you."

Jared leaned forward and pecked Jonny on the lips.

"Thanks, baby," he said gently. "Now eat up, we've got another full day ahead of us."

NOTABLY ABSENT OVER THE ENTIRE day was Trent. He didn't call either Jonny or Jared, nor asked them for any additional favors as the two spent their day in south Logan. There was a waterpark there and though it was busy, it provided a good change of scenery from the rugged coast.

After settling down on the living room couch, Jared streaming some obscure foreign movie he had little interest in, Jonny started to get a little worried about the situation. Glancing over to the wall clock, the hour was late and there was still no word or sign of Trent. Jonny hoped the cause was more missed appointments by spring break bailers, instead of what he suspected was the amount of attention the two Js had been showing each other.

With a tug of his powerful arm, Jared brought Jonny's wandering attention back on him.

"All okay?"

"Huh? Oh, yeah," Jonny replied. "I was just thinking. We're almost to the halfway point of my trip."

Jared's eyes sparked as if realizing himself for the first time.

"So, it seems we are," he replied, his words both joyous and melancholy. "Regretting anything?"

Jonny nuzzled his face against Jared's muscular neck, licking his exposed trap muscle.

"Not at all," he answered, though his eyes drifted back up toward the clock and Trent, somehow, penetrated his thoughts.

It wasn't until Wednesday afternoon that Jonny saw the elusive man for the first time since he'd swaggered off earlier in the week. Sitting alone on the balcony enjoying a good e-book, Jonny heard one of the French doors open behind him.

"What's up Jonny-boy?" said a clearly frustrated voice.

Even if he hadn't heard his familiar (and annoying) nickname, Jonny would have known who was addressing him from gruffness, not to mention the memorable cologne that drifted by on the light breeze.

Twisting, Jonny expected to see a disheveled husk; a tired and forlorn man. Instead, Trent looked a hell of a lot sexier than expected.

He was barely dressed in a low cut, white wrestling singlet that left absolutely nothing to the imagination. Thick, red lines ran down both sides of the form fitting spandex, accentuating the broad sweep of his back muscles as they tapered from his armpits down to his narrow waist.

"Well, hello there stranger," Jonny greeted, glancing at the chunky, red high tops on Trent's feet. For some reason those, coupled with his similarly striped athletic socks, were quite the turn on. "You been okay?"

"Manageable," Trent grunted, wiping his brow. His body was still pumped up from what Jonny assumed was a recent match; the new pre-workout with L-Arginine still doing its job.

Trent had mentioned offhand on the first night that he also trained himself in mixed martial arts and clients in amateur wrestling. It was something that had taken a seat on the back burner, but due to all the recent cancellations, he must've resurrected the sessions. Part of Jonny was glad that Trent hadn't shown him those areas of Swole, while another was hoping to see them one day.

For now, Jonny was left with the sight of sweat running down Trent's furry chest, his upper abs directing the beads toward the center while his fingers combed through that bushy beard, halfheartedly trying to tame it. Stepping forward, Trent's large bulge jostled to and fro as he brought himself to the railing. Turning around so his back could lean against it, every part of his body – from the package to the muscles to the veins – screamed at Jonny to help release their owner's built-up tension.

"I was getting worried about you," Jonny continued, noting where he was in the book before setting his phone down on a nearby table.

"Uh huh," muttered Trent, unconvinced. "You've been occupied well enough."

There it was, the confirmation Jonny expected to hear, though much sooner than expected.

"What do you mean?" Jonny asked, trying to buy himself a little more response time.

"You know what I mean, boyo; don't play dumb. Speaking of that, where is stubby-chubby anyway?"

"Jared? He's across town helping some guy move some furniture."

"Greg?" asked Trent. "Weird dude that likes all that ghost shit?"

"I wouldn't know," Jonny answered. "Never met the guy."

"Yeah, well, he's hot I guess. If you can look past all that stuff he talks about. What was it? Journeymen and werewolves in Goodman. Such bullshit."

Jonny shook his head, saying, "I really have no idea what you're talking about."

"Meh, it's all good. So, J-rod left you here all by yourself?" Trent continued.

He seemed to be searching for something. Jonny wasn't stupid, noticing Trent's arms were tense as he gripped the railing.

"Yeah, I guess he didn't want me to be bored while they worked. So, I'm just out here reading."

"What?" Trent asked.

"Nothing you'd be interested in; there's no pictures or pop-ups."

Trent's face soured, the wrinkle between his brows deep. Jonny remained unapologetic.

"You wouldn't be bored if you came with me," Trent told him, hoping it'd knock him down a few pegs. "I'd have made you lift that shit and earn your keep."

"No doubt you would have…"

"Damn right," Trent said proudly. "In fact, along those lines I think you owe me a workout. You've had plenty of time off."

"That's debatable…" Jonny started.

Trent cut him off mid-sentence when he bounded off the rail and in no time flat, he was standing ahead of Jonny, cologne and musk radiating off his body like heat off a hard pavement.

"Your… crotch…" Jonny sputtered. "It's… in my face."

"I know where it is," Trent said. "Just making sure you do. You're going to have a similar view later, so I want you to remember this and be ready."

"What if I don't feel like working out tonight?"

"No skin off my back," Trent replied dismissively. "If you'd rather read that little book on your little phone, so be it." He then seized Jonny's hand and smashed it against the front of his singlet. "But if you'd rather play with bigger boys and their bigger toys, then we best be heading to Swole."

"What? Right now?" said Jonny anxiously, a hefty serving of meat and potatoes right there in his clenched hand. "I... have to get ready."

Trent smirked triumphantly.

"All good; I have a few things to finish here anyway."

"Is one of those things changing out of that ridiculous outfit?" Jonny sniggered, his eyes lingering on Trent's tent since his hands had just let go.

The big guy pulsed his cock a couple times, the end becoming wet and the fabric see-through. An eyebrow was also arched, underscoring his next words.

"My action list isn't your concern, Jonny-boy. Yours however, is *all* mine. You're gonna be the one to get me out of this outfit later. So, half an hour. Your smart ass better be ready."

CHAPTER 4

FULL FLOW

"I STILL CAN'T BELIEVE YOU wore that into the mall," Jonny repeated for what had to be the fifteenth time.

Trent's Charger pulled into the Summerset Center, the red light from his gym's sign spilling into the cab as a prelude to his planned debauchery.

"They know me there," Trent answered matter-of-factly, his

serious expression holding firm like the massive thighs that jutted out from the singlet.

"Apparently, the security guard didn't know the famous Trent Cassidy all too well."

"He needs to get out more," Trent sneered, shrugging as he turned the engine off. "Could have done with some working out, too. Did you see the size of the sleeve gap he had in that shirt?"

Reaching into the back seat for his gym bag, Trent looked off into the building where a couple of women were still working out.

"Can't say I was paying all that much attention to him after he asked us to leave."

Trent laughed, opening the door. Stepping out into the parking lot, he slung the bag over his shoulder and made his way to the gym's entrance.

"You coming?"

Jonny trailed him, watching Trent strut around in that attention-seeking getup. As ridiculous as it was, it was working, Jonny hypnotically noting all the fine hairs rimmed with crimson light that edged Trent's strapping arms and legs.

"What about those people at the restaurant?" Jonny asked.

"What about them? Us boys have to eat," Trent replied. "Plus, you know from the other day that I don't give a fuck about what people think of me."

Or how you abuse hotdog buns, Jonny thought. *I'll never be able to eat them the same way again.*

Trent was first to step up from the parking lot to the sidewalk, Jonny not far behind.

"Well, what about the people at…"

"Look," Trent said abruptly as he grasped the door handle. "No matter the situation, Jonny-boy, I'd feel the absolute same way. I. Don't. Give. A. Fuck. You shouldn't so much, either."

Opening the door and going inside, high energy dance music greeted them.

"Hey there ladies," Trent said flirtatiously to two women over on his right. "It'll be closing time in about ten minutes."

They nodded with giggling smiles as their perky breasts seemed to nod in agreement. Trent carried on toward the locker rooms in the back and once he'd passed them, their eyes narrowed, locking jealously onto Jonny.

Shielding his face with a hand, he looked away, glancing into the leg room off to the left. A large man was in there, in the midst of a very heavy set of squats. He had an extremely thick and burly build, yet was obviously strong, indicated by the amount of iron he was pushing up with those tree trunk legs.

Jonny slowed his pace, watching while memories of leg day came flooding back. However, they didn't stay long, the big man yelling as the plates clanged loudly. He was done with his set and Jonny snapped his gaze back toward Trent, hoping he wasn't noticed.

"That's Will, by the way," said Trent, knowing Jonny was curious. "The weight he moves makes me nervous."

Jonny gulped at the notion of Trent being nervous of anyone, but thought better than to ask any more details.

"Shit," Trent continued, "I'm going to have to buy more plates just for that motherfucker to keep him coming here. He brings in some beastly friends to help promote the place, and I'd rather have them here versus the competition."

"*Just* for business, I presume," Jonny said.

"Yeah, and well, for some pleasure, too. But don't worry, Jonny-boy, Will doesn't swing that way and he knows not to interrupt me."

"Huh? Wait what?" Jonny asked timidly. "He's not going to be staying, is he?"

"Until he's done, yeah he will be."

What the fuck Trent? Jonny thought. *I can't even deal with the goddamn cleaning lady and you have this... beast... staying behind? He could snap me in two!*

"I... I'm not sure that I'm comfortable with..."

Trent stopped and turned, still in full view of Will in the leg room. Grabbing Jonny right on the ass, he pulled him close and kissed him. He could feel Jonny trembling in his tight hold.

"There, took care of that," Trent said, pulling away, and turning, he carried on toward the lockers. Pointing to the left again, there was another room. "We're in there tonight, so come on. Time's wasting."

Jonny just stood there, speechless. Scared to look around he ultimately glanced left.

Will was standing there in front of the squat rack, his arms resting up on the bar. All the plates were still loaded and he looked like he was about to pop a blood vessel with how much juice and pre-workout was circulating in his system.

Will didn't have to say a word, only sending a quick smirk Jonny's way. Brief as it was; it was enough to send the poor boy racing toward the locker room.

"IS THAT ALL YOU'VE GOT?" Trent barked at Jonny, whose breathing was heavy and labored.

The bar dropped, the small plates on each side bouncing a couple of times on the spongy mat.

"Damn," Trent continued. "I was expecting more from you after *two* days off. This is only the second exercise and you're already spent. Plus, we're still on baby weights."

"I don't know if you've noticed," Jonny said, "but I don't have a back like yours."

"Yet," Trent insisted, as if he were going to be his permanent trainer.

Jonny placed his hands on his hips and took in a long draw of breath, knowing he'd be heading home in just over two days.

"That was the last of those…what were they called again?"

"Deadlifts," Trent replied, removing the small weights before loading the bar up with much heavier ones.

"Yeah, those were the last deadlifts for me. They're aptly named,"

Jonny said, watching Trent bend over (still in the singlet), grip the bar, then pull it and the weights off the floor.

Trent shook slightly at the top of the movement, dropping it suddenly with a deafening racket before picking it up once more. The process repeated several more times before he grunted and shouted.

"Yeah! One set down," Trent said, wheezing at the end of it. Wiping some stray moisture from his nose with his palm, he said, "Three more to go."

Trent worked hard while Jonny got himself harder beneath his borrowed gym shorts.

Trent spied Jonny's bulge in the light gray nylon and without so much as word, moved from his last set of deadlifts right over to the lat pulldown machine.

"Sit," he ordered, pointing to the seat.

Jonny moved over cautiously, settling on the hard seat.

Trent grabbed hold of a handle on the side and pulled, the knee pad dropping against Jonny's spindly legs

"That tight enough?" Trent asked, examining Jonny in detail.

Wriggling his legs as much as he could, Jonny seemed secure.

"Yeah. I think so."

"Good, now grab hold of the bar with your palms forward. A bit wider, just outside shoulder width; there you go."

Trent was in personal trainer mode and Jonny found it super sexy to hear him talk so knowledgeably about it while showing off the results. His back was already swollen – just from the bent over rows and deadlifts – and Jonny could only imagine how much wider he was going to get by the time they finished.

"Now bring that torso back about thirty degrees," Trent instructed. "Just a little more. Good. Now as you lower the bar, using your back muscles only, breathe out until that bar touches your chest here."

A thick finger pressed against Jonny's upper chest.

Jonny began the motion, struggling a little bit to keep his back stationary.

"Only your arms should move," Trent said as Jonny held the position then returned the bar to the starting point. "Here, lemme help you."

Like a scene from someone's wet dream, Trent straddled Jonny, setting himself down on the young man. His ass ground against Jonny's cock as he got himself comfortable and for a fleeting moment, the look in Trent's eyes seemed to beg Jonny to fuck him.

"Now, pull again," Trent said before Jonny could act, placing his hands just beneath Jonny's underarms. "I'll hold you steady."

Jonny complied, lowering the bar while Trent kept him locked in place.

"Hold," Trent said, then a second later, "release."

The stack of weights slapped together at the back of the machine, signaling Trent to stand up.

"You see, that was *much* better form."

"Oh, I can see it alright," Jonny said, staring right at the front of Trent's singlet. His hard nine inches were stretching against the spandex.

Grabbing the back of Jonny's head, Trent pushed his face forward.

It was just what Jonny hoped for, opening his mouth and tilting his head so his lips could meet Trent's thick shaft. Massaging it with his mouth, he lured several prolonged groans out of Trent. His dick was salivating.

"Jesus Jonny-boy, you're a deceptive little fucker."

Jonny didn't speak, busy working the entirety of Trent with his lips. The entire front of his outfit was soon transparent from the excessive wetness of spit and precum.

Trent pulled back, stepping out from the lat machine. Grabbing hold of Jonny firmly, he pulled him over to the pull up bar.

"Stand right there," he commanded, placing Jonny beneath.

Removing the top portion of the stringer, the entirety of Trent's upper body was exposed. He then leaped, grabbing hold of the bar. Veins crisscrossed his arms and his wing-like back muscles while he hung there, and as he started to pull himself up, his dick rose to meet Jonny's mouth where the sensual, hands-free massage continued.

"Now take off my singlet," Trent said as he lowered himself.

Jonny wasted no time grabbing hold of the sides and while Trent pulled himself back up again, Jonny rolled the fabric down his torso, then hips and thighs.

Trent was free, his swollen cock slapping against the sides of Jonny's face, devoured immediately by the innocent nerd in what was one of the best blowjobs of his life.

"Lean forward more," Trent said as he watched his dick being swallowed.

Jonny listened obediently as Trent lowered himself.

Lifting himself again, Trent made sure his dick pushed Jonny's lips wide apart, followed by the walls of that warm throat.

Jonny gagged, but didn't waver, allowing the monstrous dick full access like on the incline bench during chest day. Painfully, he looked down as inches of meat disappeared down his throat, another skull fucking delivered the only way Trent knew how: rough.

A few minutes later, Trent's back muscles were burning fiercely from the pull ups while his cock and balls surged toward the point of no return.

Letting out a guttural roar that Will surely heard in the adjacent room, Trent emptied himself down Jonny's throat

Cum overflowed from the corners of his mouth, running down the young man's throbbing neck before those thick streams rolled over his chest to be sopped up by the loose tank top he wore.

TRENT DROPPED DOWN FROM THE pull up bar, stepping out from the singlet with his shoes and socks still on. Immediately, he grabbed hold of Jonny by his hard dick and led him back into the locker room.

"You're up," Trent said, and before the door had even closed, he'd stripped off what few clothes the little guy had on.

Pressing Jonny against the cold lockers, Trent kissed his neck, his beard tickling every bit of skin it encountered. Making his way down toward Jonny's nipples, he licked what remained of his own cum along the way.

Jonny gasped; Trent bit down on a nipple, hard, and then moved across to do the same to the other one.

Stepping away, Trent then looked Jonny over. Their eyes locked, his carrying the same 'fuck me' gleam he had on the lat pulldown machine. Cocking his head to the left, Trent headed for the showers, tossing his shoes and socks off to the side.

There were two individual stalls for those (normal) people who wanted some privacy, but also a larger rectangular area beyond, that Jonny was certain was for more public displays of nudity.

In the center of it was a metal cylinder with four heads attached around an upper ring, which in Jonny's twisted mind could also be used for leverage. As they both climbed onto the tiles, he couldn't shake the suspicion that Trent had this special built for whatever was about to happen.

Speaking of the devious gym owner, Trent turned on the water, sending torrents of heat cascading over their bodies. Adjusting the temperature, Trent leaned his back against the cylinder, pulling Jonny close to him.

They kissed each other beneath the hot water, both losing track of time and their surroundings as the space filled with steam.

"Fuck me," Trent whispered in Jonny's ear, his words lost in the sounds of falling water.

Jonny kept on kissing, moving his hands down toward Trent's dick.

"No," Trent said loudly, stopping him. "You. Fuck. Me… now."

He turned around, grabbing hold of the circular ring that went around the top of the shower unit. Arching his back, Trent sent his perfectly shaped ass into the stream, splashes of water dancing off its smooth curves like hundreds of tiny, spanking hands.

Jonny couldn't believe what was happening, but his cock was making zero protests about it. He moved himself forward, his erection pushing against the line between Trent's buttocks. That ass was so firm and well developed its hole was buried deep between the muscular flesh.

Grabbing a bar of soap that Jonny suspected was strategically placed earlier, he lathered up his dick and spread the suds around Trent's great divide.

"This is going to burn a little," Jonny warned.

"Bring it," Trent growled, flexing his back one more time.

The sight of each swell and striation sent Jonny to the breaking point, his shaft so engorged it felt like it could split right down the middle.

Before Jonny slid his cock between those firm cheeks, he used the bar of soap to explore the area, pushing it down toward Trent's hole. The slippery oval penetrated his ass, slowly engulfed until the entire bar disappeared inside.

"That should have greased you up enough," Jonny said. "Push it out."

He watched, and waited, but Trent's hole didn't yield.

"You come and get it," Trent challenged, immediately met by Jonny's head forcing its way in.

Soon after, Jonny could feel the bar pressed against the tip of his dick and together they advanced deeper inside.

Trent groaned, unable to contain the ecstasy caused from the burning sensation, coupled with the added length of soap being forced pleasurably further with the whole of Jonny's now well-lubed shaft.

Jonny found Trent to be incredibly tight, feeling every sensation as he moved back and forth inside his trainer. A trainer that was much bigger than he was. A trainer that was much stronger than he was. A trainer that was, for the time being, his bitch.

Jonny reveled in every fucking second of it, churning his hips into a soap-filled frenzy, his balls slapping against creamy suds, sending them running down the inside of Trent's thighs.

Each thrust brought Jonny closer to climax, so naturally he started to move faster while the splashing water made him lightheaded.

"I'm going to cum," Jonny said.

Trent immediately dropped another load onto the tile floor without the need to touch himself.

"Oh fuck…" Jonny cried, Trent's moaning doing him in. "FUCK!!!"

As Jonny pulled out, the soap bar followed. He was already spurting jets of cum, a lot of it splashing across Trent's body, pooling in an area shaped like a Christmas tree in his lower back.

"God damn!" Jonny said with reprieve, even though he was trembling at the knees.

"That was, in a word: awesome," Trent replied.

Spinning around, water ran down the length of his rippling torso, sending drops of cum falling toward the drain.

Jonny didn't pay any attention to that, because he could swear that he saw a new person standing there in front of him.

"I've not done that with anyone in a very... very long time."

"Why me of all people?" Jonny asked, truly wondering.

"I love seeing you happy," Trent said through a smirk that was becoming all too familiar. "I can't explain it, but I can feel it."

"Oh God," Jonny replied.

"What?"

"I know that look."

Trent let out a low chuckle before biting his lower lip.

"It's not always trouble."

"Most of the time it is..."

Trent struck Jonny's shoulder, then rubbed it gently.

"See!" Jonny exclaimed. "You're nothing but trouble!"

"Nah," Trent answered. "Not this time; trust me. All puns aside, you've opened me up to new things. Not going to say I like them, but if you do, then I'll try my best to."

Jonny looked confused.

"What I mean to say is: I have a proposition for you, but only if you're game."

With Trent's eyebrow arched, Jonny didn't know what to say,

speaking the first thing that came to mind.

"Okay, you have my attention. What is it that you're proposing?"

THE END